Dora saves Crystal Kingdom

adapted by Molly Reisner
based on the screenplay written by Chris Gifford
illustrated by Dave Aikins

Simon Spotlight/Nickelodeon
New York   London   Toronto   Sydney

¡Hola! I'm Dora. Today I'm reading a special story called *The Crystal Kingdom* to my friend Boots. Do you want to hear it too? Great!

Once upon a time there were four crystals that helped light the Crystal Kingdom. The yellow crystal made the sun shine yellow. The blue one made the sky and ocean blue.

The green one made the grass and trees green. And the red crystal joined the other colors to make a beautiful rainbow! The townspeople loved their colorful world.

But the king did not like sharing the crystals. "Mine, mine, mine!" said the greedy king. He used his magic wand and took all of the crystals for himself. Without the crystals, the town lost all its wonderful color! But the king would not return the crystals. Instead he hid them in other stories where no one could find them!

A brave girl named Allie wanted to rescue the crystals. She searched all over, but they were nowhere to be found.

Look! My crystal necklace is flashing! It's shining a rainbow into the kingdom where Allie lives!

Allie is flying out of her story and into our forest! She needs our help! The Snow Princess says my magic crystal will shine only if there's still color in Allie's kingdom. We have to help Allie find the crystals to keep her home shining! Will you help us too? *Fantástico!*

Hmmm . . . how will we find the crystals? Let's ask Map! Say "Map!"

Map says the yellow crystal is in *The Dragon Land Story*, the green one is in *The Butterfly Cave Story*, the blue one is in *The Magic Castle Story*, and the red crystal is in *The Crystal Kingdom Story*! We've got to jump into my storybook to get all the crystals! Say *"la primera historia"* to get us into the first story.

¡Muy bien! It worked! There are lots of dragons here. We must be in *The Dragon Land Story*. The Snow Princess has another message for us. She says to find the yellow crystal, we must save a fighting knight. *¡Vámonos!* Let's go!

There's a knight fighting a dragon! But that's a friendly dragon! We need to lasso the sword away from the knight. Backpack has a rope we can use to lasso the sword. Say "lasso" to help me lasso the sword! Good job!

The knight and dragon are happy that they stopped fighting. And the dragon knows where the yellow crystal is hidden! He saw the king put it inside a cliff. *Wheeee!* Let's fly the dragon to the yellow crystal!

Whoosh! The dragon is using his fire to blast open the cliff! We see the yellow crystal! But so does the king! He wants to steal the crystal, but the knight raises her shield and blocks his spell! Yay! We all worked together to get the yellow crystal. And the knight is giving us her shield to help us with the rest of our journey! Thanks, Knight!

Next we need to find the green crystal in *The Butterfly Cave Story.* Say *"la segunda historia"* to get us into the second story.

We're here in *The Butterfly Cave Story!* Uh-oh! My crystal is
losing color. That means color is fading from the kingdom. We've
got to get that green crystal fast! Do you see the Butterfly
Cave? *¡Vámonos!*

There's a caterpillar, and she's stuck! The Snow Princess says we can save her by shining sun into the cave. What do we have that's shiny? *¡Sí!* The shield! The sunlight is helping the caterpillar turn into a butterfly. *¡Una mariposa!* Now she can take us to the crystal!

The green crystal is inside the twelfth cocoon. Will you help us count to twelve to find it? One, two, three, four, five, six, seven, eight, nine, ten, eleven, twelve. Great! We found the green crystal. Oooh! The butterflies are hatching from the cocoons. And they're giving us each a pair of magic butterfly wings to help us on our adventure! *¡Muchas gracias!*

Now we've got to find the blue crystal in *The Magic Castle Story*. Say *"la tercera historia"* to get into the third story! *¡Muy bien!*

We made it into *The Magic Castle Story*. There's someone here who can help us! His name is Enrique, and he's a magician.

The king took Enrique's bunnies from his magic hat and put the crystal inside it. Then he locked Enrique out of the castle! We need to find five of Enrique's lost bunnies. Do you see them? Good job!

We used our butterfly wings to fly up through a castle
window! To get the crystal out of the magic hat, we have to say
"Abracadabra." Say "Abracadabra!" Yay! Allie has the yellow,
green, and blue crystals now. Enrique gives us his magic wand
to help on our adventure. *¡Gracias, Enrique!*

All we need is the red crystal to save the Crystal Kingdom! To
get us into the fourth story, say *"la cuarta historia!"*

We're in Allie's kingdom, but it's still losing color! And so is my necklace! The Snow Princess says that we have to use what we learned to get the red crystal from the king.

The greedy king has the crystal in his crown! What can we use to fly up to him? Right! Our butterfly wings! Whoa! Rocks are coming right at us! What can use to block the rocks? Yeah, the shield!

The king does not want to share his crystals. He's trying to take them from Allie with his magic wand! To break the king's spell with our magic wand, we need to say "share!" Say "share!" Yay! It worked! We got the red crystal!

The color is coming back to Crystal Kingdom! We did it! The king is surprised that we are sharing the crystals. He sees that everyone is happy, and he wants to be happy too. Wow! The king gives Allie his crown and makes her the queen! *¡La reina!*

The town is throwing a party to celebrate the return of the crystals! The king is so happy that he learned how to share. Thanks for helping us save Crystal Kingdom! We couldn't have done it without all our brave friends . . . and especially you.